ISBN 0-86163-818-2

Copyright © 1997 Award Publications Limited

First published 1997

Published by Award Publications Limited,
27 Longford Street, London NW1 3DZ

Printed in Belgium

The Little Red Train

by Hayden McAllister

illustrated by Alan Fredman

AWARD PUBLICATIONS LIMITED

Weasel Wood

It was just like any other Sunday morning on the Old Country railway line. The little red engine, still wearing his yellow nightcap, was snoozing in the Sherbert Wood railway shed.

Jack, his driver, was sitting nearby. He had just finished making a toy model of the red engine. "All this toy needs now is a nightcap," Jack said with a chuckle. "Then it will look exactly like the little red engine!"

A little further down the line, Ben Bear, Stephanie Squirrel and Reggie Rabbit were busy washing a railway carriage.

Half an hour later, the sound of strange voices woke the little red engine. When he opened his eyes he could hardly believe what he saw.

There was a circus clown and an Indian chief talking to Jack the engine driver. Ben Bear, Reggie Rabbit and Stephanie Squirrel were all listening so the red engine listened too.

"Big Chief Mountain Eagle is looking for his daughter," Carrie Clown was saying. "She must have got out of the bus at our last stop, and nobody noticed."

"What shall I do?" asked Big Chief Mountain Eagle, looking very sad. "Little Brown-Eyes and I were due to sail back across the great water to America today. We've been touring with the circus and now we're going home."

"We've searched Badger Bank for her," went on Carrie Clown. "Our circus bus was passing along Badger Bank when we noticed that Little Brown-Eyes was missing. We've also searched Dingle Dell, but there's no sign of Little Brown-Eyes there either."

"Mmm. So that only leaves Weasel Wood," Jack said thoughtfully, stroking his chin.

"Yes," said Carrie Clown. "But the Mayor of Weasel Wood said he wouldn't let us search there. So we wondered if you could do anything to help us."

"Well, there is a railway line running through Weasel Wood," said Jack. "But no trains have passed that way for many years."

"But if there are railway tracks there, why no railway trains?" asked Big Chief Mountain Eagle.

"Because Grey Weasel, the Mayor of Weasel Wood, has stopped all trains passing through the wood," said Jack, climbing aboard the red engine. "But the little red engine and I will certainly risk going there now. In fact we'll do anything we can to help you find Little Brown Eyes. Come on, everyone."

So ten minutes later, the little red train was rattling along the Old Country railway line. The red engine was very keen to help Big Chief Mountain Eagle find his missing daughter.

Jack was shovelling lots of coal into the furnace, and at the Dingle Dell bend he sounded the steam whistle. "*Phweep-phweep*!" went the little red engine as it raced through Dingle Dell.

"Wowwee! I've never seen the little red train going so fast – and on a Sunday too!" gasped Mopsie Mole, who was watching from a fence. "It's going so fast it's blown my best hat away!"

Carrie Clown, Reggie Rabbit, Stephanie Squirrel and Ben Bear were all on board the red train as it sped towards Badger Bank.

Ben Bear was leaning out of a carriage window, gazing through his binoculars. He was hoping he might spot Little Brown-Eyes. But all he could see were trees and grass and an old badger with a walking-stick.

Big Chief Mountain Eagle was travelling with Jack in the engine cab.

"What is Little Brown-Eyes wearing?" asked Jack.

"A brown dress. She also wears a big red feather in her hair," said Mountain Eagle. "It is the same colour as the red engine!"

Weasel Wood was not a pleasant place. No flowers grew there because the Mayor of Weasel Wood didn't like flowers. Mayor Grey Weasel liked grey scarves, so all the weasels who lived there had to wear grey scarves.

Near the edge of Weasel Wood there was a big picture of Mayor Grey Weasel blocking the railway line ahead.

Jack stopped the red train and called to a small rabbit hiding at the base of a tree. "Have you seen a little Indian girl with a red feather in her hair?" he asked.

"Yes, she went into Weasel Wood an hour ago," whispered the little rabbit.

"But how will we get past Mayor Grey Weasel's picture?" asked Mountain Eagle.

"I'll have to drive the little red engine right through the picture," cried Jack. "Hang on tightly, everyone!"

Five minutes later the little red train steamed into the heart of Weasel Wood. Carrie Clown and the animals gazed anxiously out of the carriage windows. Everything looked very grey.

Jack leaned out of the window, looking for any sign of Little Brown-Eyes. "I'll call her," he said and shouted, "Little Brown-Eyes!" at the top of his voice. But there was no reply.

Then, right ahead, the wood suddenly opened up.

Jack could see a bend in the track ahead, and part of a small hill. Then he grew very worried because he could see puffs of smoke appearing over the hill.

"There must be another train – coming towards us!" gasped Jack as he pulled the brake handle.

"Perhaps this Grey Weasel has a grey railway engine?" suggested Mountain Eagle.

"We'll soon find out!" said Jack, as the little red engine puffed slowly round the bend.

But it wasn't a railway train after all, it was Little Brown-Eyes sending smoke signals! She had been hoping someone would see them and come to rescue her. Everyone cheered at the sight of her. She was so happy to see her father again. And Big Chief Mountain Eagle was overjoyed to find his daughter.

"Would you still like to catch your ship back to America?" asked Jack. "We can go directly to Seagull Harbour from here."

"That would be a perfect ending to a day full of many strange twists and turns!" said Mountain Eagle, smiling broadly.

The little red train arrived at Seagull Harbour in good time. On the clifftop the happy friends could see the Seagull lighthouse.

"Your friendship and help to us have been as bright and clear as the beams of light from that lighthouse!" said Mountain Eagle.

"This red feather is all I have," said Little Brown-Eyes to Jack. "But please take it, along with my thanks to all of you, and especially to the little red engine."

Jack smiled and walked over to the little red engine. From the cab he took the toy model of the red engine, which he brought back and gave to the delighted Little Brown-Eyes.

An hour later, the ship carrying Big Chief Mountain Eagle and Little Brown-Eyes had started on its way across the great water, back to America.

Waving goodbye from the clifftop were Jack, Carrie Clown, Ben Bear, Stephanie Squirrel and Reggie Rabbit.

On the railway track behind them stood the little red engine. He was sending special heart-shaped smoke signals to Little Brown-Eyes, which he knew she would understand.

"Well," said Jack, after a while. "We'd better set off for home soon. But don't worry, my friends, we'll travel back by the Clickitty-Clack railway track – so we'll miss Weasel Wood by miles!"

The Naughty Elephant

The front of the red engine was open. Jack was working inside the boiler with a spanner, trying to fix a broken pipe. The little red engine's face was all screwed up. "I feel as if I'm at the dentist's!" he groaned.

"Don't worry, old chum," soothed Jack. "We'll soon have you as right as rain. Then we'll be off to Jumbo Junction to pick up Ellie Elephant. We have to take her to Happy Meadow Circus."

"Ooh, I hope they sell candy-floss," said the little red engine.

Soon the little red engine was ready. Jack and Ben Bear hitched the truck on to the engine, Jack blew the steam whistle, and off they went.

When they arrived at Jumbo Junction, Ellie Elephant was already dressed in her circus outfit and eagerly awaiting them.

"She looks a nice friendly elephant," said Jack, as Reggie Rabbit and Stephanie Squirrel led her towards the little red train. "I only hope she will fit into our brand-new railway truck!"

Ellie did fit into the red truck, but it was a very tight squeeze!

Ben Bear, Reggie Rabbit and Stephanie Squirrel had joined Jack in the engine cab. "We'll have to chug along very slowly, my friends," he told them, "because on our way to Happy Meadow Circus we have to pass over Bumpity Bank!"

But even before they reached Bumpity Bank there were problems. Ellie Elephant was too big to go under Squeaker Bridge. She almost went under . . . but not quite.

"Ellie is too big for the bridge!" declared Reggie Rabbit.

"No! The bridge is too small for Ellie!" argued Stephanie Squirrel.

"If only it was a rubber bridge," said Ben Bear, "we could squeeze Ellie under it . . ."

Jack said nothing. He was standing on the top of the bridge, thinking very hard about what he could do, when Ellie suddenly reached up with her trunk and lifted Jack's cap off his head. Then she put it on her own head!

"We'll just have to get Ellie out of the truck and walk her round the bridge," said Jack. "I can't think of any other way."

But when the railway animals tried to get Ellie to climb out of the truck, she just would not budge! They pushed her and they pulled her but she wouldn't move.

Then two friendly pigs appeared, carrying pulleys and ropes. They proudly declared that they could lift Ellie Elephant out of the railway truck!

"Well, you can certainly try," said Jack. "And thank you for offering to help. But please, be very, very careful."

So the two pigs tried, oh, how they tried! They heaved and they wheezed, they heaved and they huffed, and they heaved and they puffed . . . But they couldn't lift Ellie Elephant out of the truck, so in the end they gave up and set off for home.

Then, suddenly, even before Jack could cry, "Hey! Stop that!" Ellie had jumped out of the truck! She raced around in a big circle, then ran back on to the railway track and, still wearing Jack's cap, she began to run away.

"Whoa there!" roared Ben Bear.

"Stop!" cried Jack.

"*Pwheep-PWHEEP*!" went the red engine.

"Oh dear, oh dear, oh dear!" chorused Stephanie Squirrel and Reggie Rabbit, because they knew that Ellie Elephant was heading straight towards Bumpity Bank!

Jack and the railway animals quickly jumped on board
the little red train and gave chase.
    But by now, Ellie Elephant was thoroughly enjoying herself!
She ran happily down the railway track, and as she approached
Bumpity Bank she ran faster and faster.

Jack put on as much speed as he dared and tried to catch the elephant, but it was too late! As Ellie reached the first part of Bumpity Bank, she ran clean off the track and disappeared into the fields below.

Jack tried to slow down the little red engine. The brakes screeched, but they didn't stop the red train from going uppity-down, uppity-down, on the bumpity humps of Bumpity Bank.

"Yippee! It's like being on the big dipper!" squeaked Stephanie Squirrel.

"I hope we don't go any faster," gasped Reggie Rabbit. "Or we'll run clean off the tracks – just like Ellie Elephant!"

"We must try and catch Ellie Elephant!" cried Ben Bear. "But I can't see her anywhere!" He picked up his binoculars.

Then, in the distance, he caught sight of Ellie, racing across a field. In the middle of the field, standing next to a duckpond, was a big wooden platform.

On top of the platform was Mayor Grey Weasel. He was making a speech through a megaphone and was shouting, "Ban all flowers from the countryside! Vote for the one and only Mayor Grey Weasel!" And at that very moment Ellie Elephant knocked over the platform and sent Mayor Grey Weasel flying – *SPLOSH*! – head-first into the duckpond!

Three minutes later, after going through a long tunnel, the railway friends saw Ellie again. She had joined another railway line and was moving, like them, towards Cross-Line Junction.

"We must try and stop Ellie at this junction!" cried Jack to the little red engine. "Because if we don't, she will end up running all the way to Waterloo station!"

The little red train suddenly steamed ahead in a mighty effort to get in front of Ellie Elephant, and just beyond Cross-Line Junction Jack slammed on the brakes.

As Ellie Elephant lumbered towards them, she wavered and wobbled and finally slowed right down.

When Reggie Rabbit, Stephanie Squirrel and Ben Bear saw Ellie plodding towards them, they opened the door of the railway truck and Ellie Elephant climbed back on board!

"*Pwheep-pwheep*!" the little red engine cried triumphantly.

Jack mopped his brow. "Come on, my friends," he said. "Let's take Ellie to Happy Meadow Circus before she gets us into any more mischief!"

Ben Bear, Reggie Rabbit and Stephanie Squirrel spent the rest of the journey chatting with Ellie, so when they finally arrived at Happy Meadow Circus they were all good friends.

Once they'd delivered Ellie to the circus-master, Jack and the railway animals stood beside the little red engine and ate some candy-floss. The red engine ate some too!

Of course, everyone knows that little red engines don't really eat candy-floss, but please don't forget . . . this little red engine is just that little bit special.

"*Phweep-phweep!*"